The
Animal
Congress
or
Of Human
Behavior

Elpidio Gracia

FootePrint Press
California, USA

Published by FootePrint Press.

This book is a work of fiction. Any references to historical events, real peo-ple, or real locales are used fictitiously and are not meant to depict actual events or change the fictional nature of the work. Any other resemblance to persons, living or dead, is entirely coincidental.

Publisher's Cataloging-In-Publication Data

Names: Gracia, Elpidio.

Title: The Animal Congress or Of Human Behavior/ Elpidio Gracia.

Description: [Manteca], California, USA : FootePrint Press, [2021]

Identifiers: LCCN 2021937154 | ISBN 978-0-9904353-4-1

Table of Contents

Prologue

The events of which you will read in this narrative having occurred, my chief interest concerns whether in some future day the story could be rewritten from the point of view of that future generation. My cousin, Timothy Mouse, who was a destructive baby when the story began is my only assistant. My mind is completely blank. I have no constructive thoughts on the matter. I said I suspect that my apprentice knows the answer, but he will not tell me.

One day, to test his perceptions, I propounded three enigmas relative to animal behavior. "Timothy," I asked him, "tell me which animal do you think would respond in the way I'm going to mention. First, if one of its legs is caught in a trap, it would rather lose its limb than to be caught."

Timothy was standing in front of my desk, his hands in his pockets. He was wearing navy blue trousers. His white shirt with blue pin stripes was accented by a navy blue bow tie with polka dots. His loafers were cordovan. The large frame glasses made him look quite intellectual. His attire enhanced his over-all appearance because he was quite small, even for a mouse.

Timothy thought deeply for a while and then said, "A bird?"

"Wrong," I said to him with a certain impatience.

"Second, if its young are threatened by a predator it will forsake them in order to save its own life."

Once again Timothy consulted his mind and heart before answering, "The tiger."

"Wrong again!" I scolded him. "Timothy, where is your mind? Think!"

I could see no evidence of shame on his part. Barnyard animals who were born in Illinois do not usually know about tigers at any rate.

"Third," I continued with my typical false patience, "what bird has the reputation of stealing other birds' nests?"

"Oh, that's easy," replied Timothy because he had helped me compile the information for this manuscript. "The hen."

"Three times wrong!" I screeched. "Timothy how will you help me re-write the chronicle?"

"Oh," he said shrugging his shoulders. "I just don't have social antennas, I guess." And he went off whistling.

It was that remark which made me think he had the answer after all.

By the way, Timothy is the son of Cassandra and Harold Mouse. I am not sure if I am his cousin on his mother's or his father's side, or if I am a cousin at all.

Miguel Bookmouse

20__

Chapter One

Why Didn't I Listen to My Mother?

Cassandra Mouse took a seat on the bluff that overlooked the deep place in the creek and strained to keep from sobbing. Had she really left? Did her husband understand that she meant to return after traveling? Or would he look for a younger mouse to take her place? As she thought, revenge loomed large in her heart.

"May he take a young rat by mistake! A young rat who will grow so big that she will crowd him out of house and hole," she said aloud. *Those disgusting beasts,* she thought and shivered. *Too bad they look so much like us. Likely men make war on mice because they mistake us for them.*

She thought about Cousin Lemuel. Just three months before, in December, while looking for loose corn in the barn, he had come upon a rat trap.

Lemuel was young and inexperienced. He had only been born in October. His mother, Cassandra's aunt, had taught him about mouse traps. They even had a mouse trap in their hole–for they lived in the barn. She used it to teach her children to recognize and run around traps in real life. There were regular drills. However, the rat trap was so much bigger that Lemuel never suspected danger. He claimed that the damp, cold air and fear of the cat had dulled his senses when all of a sudden, he saw a looming platform, unlike any that he had ever seen before, and his curiosity got the best of him.

It had been a struggle to get up on top, and he triggered it. Fortunately, because he was so small, the great metal bar passed right over him, catching only the tip of his tail, and allowing him to escape from its clutches.

Just then a young rat loomed over him. Lemuel almost died of a heart attack because he thought it was the cat. He crouched and squealed and waited, for his mother had warned him that cats play with their victims before doing the unthinkable. However, no claw pricked his tender hide.

Instead he heard a voice speaking to him. "Don't be afraid little brother," it said. The accent was almost offensive. "If you think I'm that old cat, you're mistaken. I'm as afraid of that old critter as you are, although I'll be much bigger than you when we both grow up. I'm Stacey, son of the barnyard rat."

"Rat?" Lemuel shuttered. All his fears of and prejudices against rats were excited again in him. It was almost as bad as being caught by the cat!

He lay there as if dead.

"Get up. Get up quick," coaxed Stacey. "That cat is afoot. But you saved my life. I had completely forgotten everything the rats taught me. All I saw was the cheese. I was headed straight for it when you sprang the trap. I'll always be grateful to you Little Brother. Now run."

And run they did. The rat took a trail known to him, and Lemuel barely made it down his hole when a furry gray man almost threw itself against the barnyard wall.

Lemuel was so scared that he left a small puddle. Kneeling on the safe side of the wall, he trembled and cried as the cat scratched angrily outside.

The aunt had related the account with many details to her sister, Cassandra's mother. Mixed with fear and relief, there was also a fair amount of indignation. Mice suffered because of rats, but the rats considered themselves their brothers. It appears that Stacey thought Lemuel sprang the trap on purpose to save him.

It would serve that old mouse right if he married a young rat! Cassandra thought and she felt some consolation. A faint smile crept across her face.

"I can't go home—not just yet. He screamed at me. I've got my pride. After all, I am a person. A mouse person, that is. But if I am to travel, I must have a fitting companion. Maybe a respectable animal widow woman. One who can be out of the house for several weeks."

She sat there lost in thought. It was March, and although the day was unseasonably warm, the night would be cold. It was maybe 2 o'clock. The sun was high in the sky and warmed her because there were few leaves on the trees.

However, the sunlight would start to fade within three hours, and in five hours complete darkness would cover the field. Cassandra was pensive. Although she, like all mice, was blessed with night vision, Cassandra, personally, was terrified of the dark.

Just then a hard, bony hand half pushed her. Looking down first, she saw two orange webbed feet. Looking up, she perceived that the "hand" was not a hand at all but a duck's bill.

"What have we here?" asked the duck, talking to herself. She was about to lift the mouse up by the tail, but held back for fear of taking liberties. Her mother had often emphasized to her children how they should behave with strangers. She was honest enough to admit her impertinence.

"I would have picked you up by the tail to see you better since you're no bigger than a frog, but I saw mother telling me I better not." She stared intently at the tiny gray creature who was between her feet.

"You did?" squeaked Cassandra.

"I did?" asked the duck. "Did what?"

"Where is your mother, if you saw her?"

"I saw her in my mind, silly! In my mind. Don't you understand metaphors?"

"Metaphors are illustrations," said the mouse, terrified at the thought of one duck's lifting her up by the tail or of being caught in a fight between two of them.

"Be it a metaphor or a saying, what I meant was that my mother insisted that we always respect the dignity of other animals." She carefully shifted her large flat feet so as to not trample the tiny mouse underfoot and lowered herself down beside her.

Now Cassandra could see the duck up close. She noted to herself that the mallard's mottled feathers were similar to a chicken's feathers, but somewhat different, since ducks swim and chicken do not.

The air was starting to take on a chill and the mouse drew nearer to the duck in hopes of half-hiding herself among the brownish feathers. Would this great creature be her traveling companion? That would be more than she had hoped for. Ducks do not seem to feel the cold, but mice do. Also, mice drown while ducks can swim. On the back of her living boat she could cross creeks, ponds, and even rivers.

"Do you like to travel?" asked the mouse, who felt it was better on this occasion to be direct and not beat around the bush.

"I have traveled as far as the rapids on the other side of the bridge," the duck answered with great pride.

The trip to the "rapids" by water or by land would have been an adventure for Cassandra. The place which the duck called "the rapids," where the creek narrowed and fairly leaped over several big stones, was at least half a mile away and completely out of sight because of the bend in the creek and the woods. For Cassandra, it might as well have been the other side of the world.

"But I shouldn't go there often, because ducks that swim that far often never return."

"What happens to them?" asked Cassandra.

"Foxes, I think," replied the duck, who then mentioned her friend Hans, whom she was supposed to marry.

Mrs. Mouse's eyes became quite large. "You mean the man–I mean the duck–you were supposed to marry"–but the words were held back by a strong urge to cry and a fragile sense of decency.

The duck understood and nodded her head. Then, after debating within herself whether to say more, she said it anyway. "Don't worry yourself about him. He was always impetuous."

"Oh, how selfish I am," bemoaned the poor mouse, and she related the story of how she had quarreled with her husband and left him and their young son behind to see the world if only she could find a suitable traveling companion. As the tears flowed, she also told about Cousin Lemuel's narrow escape and declared on no uncertain terms how she felt about rats.

It was as if two hearts met, for they had much in common.

"Look," said the duck after thinking it over a minute or two. "That mouse can take care of himself and the boy while we travel. I'll see that you get back safely. Riding on my back, no one will mistake you for a frog."

The duck's tendency to constantly compare her to a frog or to associate her with a frog put a damper on Cassandra's feelings, and therefore on her desire to spend a lot of time with her aquatic friend. Was it not rumored among the other animals that ducks and geese sometimes abandon their nests and hens have to incubate them? (Hens do not eat mice. They simply peck at their tails.) And how had the duck attracted her attention in the first place, if not by pecking her?

Instantly a cold feeling, even colder than an early spring day, came over her, almost overwhelming her.

The duck crooked her neck down and around in order to better see her new friend.

"I'll call you, Froggy, since I can't help but think of a frog when I look at you." Then she winked.

"And you? What shall I call you?" asked the disheartened mouse.

"You can call me what I am. Duck."

Mrs. Mouse felt quite uncomfortable now. She was beginning to suspect that if she tried to beg off or free herself the duck would not let her go. After all, she had placed herself under the duck's feathers. No one had obligated her to do that. And as she pulled out from within her soft, warm refuge, the duck's massive head was blocking her escape.

Oh dear, why didn't I listen to my mother? thought Cassandra, very distressed. *She always said that it takes time to form friendships and that friends who immediate-*

ly become possessive are not true friends. I can only con-clude that this duck is not my true friend. She has even changed my identity. Next, she will expect me to swim like a frog!

At that moment, a splash was heard in the water be-low and the duck lifted up her head instinctively. She looked piercingly at the water and lifted herself up, turn-ing her head to the side. Stealthily she waddled down the slopping embankment, her head and neck parallel to the ground and without a sound entered the water. Noiselessly she glided upon its surface observing intently something of which only she was conscious. Then, quick and direct as an arrow, her head plunged into the water and came up with a tiny frog in its mouth.

The mouse looked in horror as her new-found friend struggled with the hapless creature until she had over-powered it. She watched as the duck swallowed the frog in one piece. Then she saw the duck crawl out of the water and head up the bank again. Although the fright-ened mouse scampered away, she could not really run faster than the duck, who was much larger than she. The web-footed animal ran up the slope at great speed, while the mouse barely had the advantage of a fifty-foot head start. She rounded a mound of stones and hid herself among them, just in time to get out of sight. She trusted that if there were any snakes, they would be sleeping.

The duck ran frantically to and fro, looking for her prisoner, for prisoner indeed she considered the small rodent. She went pecking here and there with great fury for she was a self-willed individual. Only when it was almost dark did she abandon the quest and retreat to the home for the barnyard fowl where they had made a place for her. She was a lone duck among many chickens.

Cassandra made herself comfortable in her new hole. She was afraid to go out into the night and embarrassed to go home anyway. Comfortable, it may be said, although in fact, she was terrified.

Chapter Two

Trouble Was Brewing

After Cassandra's exit, Byron thought it only right that he should leave too. A dejected Harold Mouse and his little boy bade him farewell.

"Come back if you can't find any other place. Remember, it wasn't your fault. It wasn't anybody's. Not really."

Byron restrained himself from looking back because a tear—or two or three—was blinding him. How pleasant his stay with the Mouses had been, at least at first. They had talked about things which are important to men. Everything from how to repair leaks in the roof to how to help animals cope with rejection. His spirits had been lifted even if they had not reached any definite conclusions. He did not feel so bad being a worm, or worse yet, being called a snake.

"It's not always bad being mistaken for a snake, anyway," he mused as he glided up the passageway that led to the landing among the piled stones which sheltered the entrance to the Mouses' abode.

"Once, a young bird thought that I was a small snake and raised such a commotion that his mother came. Of course, the mother knew the difference between an earthworm and a snake. At any rate, all that squawking had befuddled her, giving me time to escape into the earth."

Having reached the clearing before the doorway from which the mice peeked out to make sure there was no danger, he rested. For mice, danger is always present. Cats. Dogs. Snakes. Boys.

It was half past one, and the day was warm. Light filtered through openings between the stones, casting a pattern like a crocheted scarf on the damp earth. Byron kept thinking. *What a confusion! Worms open passages in the earth so that air and water can enter. Therefore, they are good. But if they get up on the back porch, they are not good. Snakes are good because they eat mice...*

That bitter thought made him wince because Harold Mouse and his son Timothy were now his best friends. Maybe that was why most worms bitterly resent being called snakes. Men say that mice and rats are bad because they multiply fast and eat up all their food. Byron knew that was an exaggeration. Rats eat little and mice, even less. But when rats or mice get into a bag of flour or cornmeal, men throw the rest away. It's true that rats and mice have similar customs. For that reason, rats consider mice their brothers, but no mouse, it appears, wants to be called a rat.

Byron promised himself not to rest until he had resolved that mystery. The only thing he knew for sure was that he felt good after the morning spent with the mouse family. That was a beginning. But of what?

He looked both ways before going out among the blades of grass, cut short and withered because of the cold winter. By keeping very close to the ground, probably no bird would notice him. Many had not yet arrived from the southern migrations anyway. Dogs and cats didn't bother about him very much (with the exception of kittens and puppies). And, thankfully, it wasn't yet fishing season.

What he really wanted was to be treated, not like a worm or a snake, but like a man. No, he didn't want to be a man, that is, human. Humans had their own share of problems, to be sure. For example, his keen senses told him that the day was drawing to a close. Darkness was coming and it would be cold. If he were human, he would have a problem. What to eat? Where to sleep? What to put on? But being an earthworm, he only had to bore a hole in the ground and sleep. What could be simpler? He really liked that better.

Then again, humans get so confused. He remembered the amusement of all the animals when the humans who lived on their lot mistook the very tracks which they had left in the soft earth for those of intruders.

It seemed that the biggest boy was wearing his father's boots and carrying a cane. The smaller came pulling his little red wagon with the small dog atop. Granny followed while the great dog leaped and jumped, making circles around them. The only thing is that in jumping from the path, he landed on the grass where he left no footprints and then ran over the tracks he had already made.

When the parents saw the tracks, they concluded that an old man who supported himself on a cane had passed along on the north side of their property too close for comfort. Analyzing the evidence, they concluded that the old man was followed by his son, who, in turn was followed by the wife, pushing the baby carriage. All evidence indicated that this company had two large dogs.

Of course, the tracks did not indicate that the vehicle—a wagon and not a baby carriage—was being pulled and not pushed. And Granny apparently forgot about their outing. But of course, most of the time Granny was confused about just about everything.

At any rate, fear, doubt, and mistrust festered in the man's heart and he inquired everywhere as to who could have left those tracks. Then someone mentioned a camp of wandering people who had camped along the stream about a few miles on the other side of the "rapids." The man, whom they called Felix, went to spy on them, pretending to be selling eggs and saw a family that could have answered that description.

The family head was, not an old man but a younger one, who walked on crutches. He had four children, three girls and one boy, instead of two. But he did have two dogs.

Felix was convinced that they were the ones, and he denounced them to the police. He even claimed that about that time eggs had disappeared from the hen house and that either the man—or more probably his thieving children—had stolen them, or the dogs had eaten them.

All the neighborhood began to team up against the "outsiders." Caravans of cars streamed up and down the main highway and returned by the dirt road which lay to the east of the campsite until the wanderers got the message and left. The police had already warned them that they could not restrain the mob and, therefore, would not be responsible for what happened. (That could be stricken from the historical records only if the villagers apologized, I suppose.)

It's not so bad being a worm, thought Byron. *It's being called a 'lowly earthworm' or a snake. That's what bothers me to no end.*

But the story did not end there. For six successive days, the two boys, Granny, and the dogs went out, leaving fresh tracks every time. When they "discovered" their tracks, they had fresh reason to believe the intruders had returned. But by the seventh day, a fair-minded person told them that the traveling band had left the area four days before and that it was impossible that they were leaving fresh tracks.

Then customers began to comment that Felix's hens had not been laying so much lately and that they had been forced to go to the store in town, causing some to wonder if Felix even had any eggs to steal? Then the right front wheel came off of the red wagon, but the three kept parading anyway. Of course, it left different tracks, and the error was discovered.

Felix, until the end of his days, said the "robbers" had left the first tracks and that his children and dogs were simply imitating them. For that he became the laughing-stock of humankind and animalkind alike.

No, no, thought Byron. *It's not so bad being a worm after all.*

Underground, there was a lot of activity. Earthworms were working furiously to prepare the earth for men's sowing. From time to time a plow cut a worm in two and some said that each half kept living. But Byron had his doubts about that. The problem was that the head part could grow a new tail. But many worms to whom that happened cried out, "Jubilation! I'm free! I'm a new person! I'm a new worm!" And they headed off for new parts, turning their backs on house and home. Byron had lost his father and a couple of cousins in that way. His mother had always said, "Don't go up so near the surface when you hear the roar of the tillers or feel their rumbling."

But Father always said, "Be quiet, Woman. Are you correcting me?"

Byron feared that he had inherited some of that stubbornness from his father's side. They were always the ones that got mangled by the plow or got caught for fishing. Other worms said it did not have to end that way, but that is the way it was, especially with Byron's kin.

As he crawled along, he reviewed the good and the bad of what he had seen and learned.

Grass—even, short, dried; ground cold: "Probably no one would run the lawn mower that day."

Day—grayish and cool: "Not many birds. Yet."

Shadow of a bird (not a hawk): "Begin to burrow."

Hawk's shadow: "No birds. Keep going."

Mother taught that, and several relatives on her side of the family had the same insight. But Father? "Nobody tells me how to live my life." And he was cut in two.

It's true that worms do not grieve like mice do when a family comes to a bad or tragic end. At the same time, the survival instinct is strong in all—both in humans and in animals.

He crawled along steadily. The sun was already getting lower in the sky and the light becoming dimmer. He heard the furious tirades of the duck on the other side of the wire fence and reasoned that although danger was only about fifty feet away, the fence was his temporary protection. Also, the duck did not know of his presence.

What he did not know is that the duck was looking for Cassandra (and for what purpose).

He crawled steadily along. His goal was to reach the vicinity of the barn and burrow down into the warmer earth against its western side where the sun had bathed it all afternoon. As he neared the barn, he became aware of activity that he would have to jot down in his journal of animal behavior.

A fat rat ran along, pursued by the fluffy gray cat. When the cat had almost overtaken him, another rat, a sleek one, intercepted. This confused the cat, who began to pursue the second rat. Just in time, a third rat came on the scene and the furry feline went after him.

Felix, the farmer, witnessed it all and loudly announced that he would declare war on all ratdom. He entered the house and returned quickly with his shotgun. As he fired, the first rat trampled Byron. Obviously, he had not seen him, for there is neither friendship nor ill-will between rats and worms. His bullet missed the rat but hit the earth about a foot from where Byron was. Mother had not told him what to do in times like this.

The rats quickly disappeared into the barn and the bewildered cat ran in circles like a kitten who plays with its own tail.

"Poison doesn't work with them," growled Felix. "They play with my traps as if they did exercises with them in their holes. They can actually remove the cheese without springing the trap."

The man paced as frantically as the cat did, as humans tend to do when they are upset.

"I know!" he said with the snap of his fingers. "Traps that don't look like traps and more cats. I'm going to leave this one in the woods near a farmhouse. Maybe they'll adopt him."

With that, he grabbed the cat by the lose skin on the back of his neck and threw him onto the seat of his pick-up.

As the truck was pulling out of the barnyard, Byron was boring down into the earth beside the barn beneath a large stone that had been left there.

It was obvious that trouble was brewing.

Chapter Three

Convince Them to Change Their Strategy

The knock on the door raised Harold's spirits. He hurried to open it.

"So, you decided to return," he was about to say, when he realized that the visitor was not Byron the worm at all, but his cousin, Miguel Bookmouse. He was surprised because Miguel did not have the custom to visit him.

"Come in," he invited after an awkward pause. Miguel sensed that his cousin was expecting someone else.

Miguel was a reporter, investigator, and avid reader, as his name suggested. In English, he would be called "Bookworm," which did not really suit him as a name. But in Spanish he would be called "the library mouse." Since "Bookmouse" sounded more genteel than "Library Mouse," an ancestor of his had legalized the former name. There were also secondary advantages in bearing that name. From one generation to another it could evolve from "Bookmouse" to "Bookmas" and then to "Bukmas" and thus not attract so much attention to the fact that he was a mouse. His cousin's plain last name "Mouse" did not have the same versatility. For that reason, Harold harbored a certain ill-will against his relative.

The Mouses' hole was cozy. Harold and his wife had "papered" the walls with leaves and tiny flowers. The "carpet" was moss mowed to a thin layer which evenly covered the floor and it looked like a carpet in the finest homes of men. Two overstuffed chairs were against one wall and a large sofa was against the opposite wall. On the low table which was in the middle of the room were scraps and bits of paper which Harold used for chronicling the events of the vicinity. Try as he might, he could not conquer the mouse tendency to shred paper into bits. Other mice even used shredded paper to carpet their floors.

On the wall was a sketch of his family tree. A very prolific group they were. A human's family is significantly different from a mouse's. Men's family trees usually have only one trunk. Mice's family trees are patterned after that tree in India which develops into a forest. As the branches extend, something like runners or vines drop down and take root in the ground, forming a secondary or dependent tree. Miguel, whom Harold called Michael, could not help noticing that the branch or tree which represented his family had been chopped down and uprooted.

Harold prepared a pot of tea and put cakes on the

table and waited for Miguel to explain the purpose of his call.

"Are you aware of all that is going on in our immediate world?" he asked as he folded his paws upon his chest.

"I'm not sure if I am," replied Harold.

"The farmer has declared open warfare on the rats, of which there are many. This will have tragic results for us unless we can convince the rats to change their strategy."

"What do you mean?" asked Harold. "Convince them to change their strategy?"

Miguel gave himself time to think the answer out. "It would be better to say 'change their attitude,' I think. Do you understand what I'm trying to say?"

Harold shrugged his shoulders. "Not exactly. I try to think as little about rats as possible. I suppose 'strategy' and 'attitude' mean about the same thing. But how can that be achieved?"

Miguel sipped his tea. "This tea is very good. How did you manage to get into the man's house to bring it without the cat's seeing you?"

Harold almost jumped up at that question, but before he could answer, Miguel asked, "Where's Cassandra?"

The second question was even more alarming because the truth was, he did not know. Traveling, he supposed. He stammered, "She went out for a while."

Then he realized that one reason he wanted it to be Byron who arrived was that Byron knew why his wife had gone and, therefore, he would not have to explain anything to him.

"I imagine she's out to bring food," said Miguel, not waiting for an explanation. "But I didn't see her at the Mouse Storehouse. Did she go to the Main House? You know, first of all, how dangerous that would be for her personally. Also, you know that the rats have said that if mice can enter the house, they can too. It's very important that all mice cooperate by not going near the house. We want to give the impression that we disappeared."

Harold knew that his wife had not gone to the house and that she had not brought the tea from there either. But he thought it would be wise not to contradict Cousin Michael. He simply changed the subject.

"What attitude of rats do we need to change?" asked Harold.

It annoyed Miguel very much that Harold did not answer his question, and he decided to resort to one-up-manship. Nevertheless, he tried to control his emotions.

"Their defiance. They don't accept that they can't win in a war against men. Nevertheless, they are organizing demonstrations and even talk of raids on the farmer's house."

Harold sat up straight in his chair. "Such action would spell the death of all us rodents," he exclaimed. "What can we do?"

"We've got to talk to the rats, reason with them that what they're doing is unwise," declared Miguel with all the conviction he could muster.

The conversation rambled on for a while, at times almost without cause or purpose. Each had to carefully select words or ideas that did not provoke or irritate the other unnecessarily. It was tiring.

In the midst of such deliberations and diplomatic affirmations, a noise exploded and the ground shook.

"What can that be?" Harold gasped and ran straight through the front door and up the short tunnel which led to his front porch. Miguel followed on his heels.

Peeking through the opening, Harold saw the trail Byron had blazed through the grass. He saw the smoke that resulted from the gunfire. The rats had gone, but the farmer was there, scolding the cat.

"Byron! What has happened to Byron?" Harold squealed and was about to dart out in full sight of the farmer and the cat when his cousin caught him by one of his hind legs.

"Let me go! Let me go!" he protested, but Miguel held fast.

"No, no. Don't be rash, Cousin. Listen! Think! Would the man be shooting at an earthworm? Most probably he was shooting at rats, even though we don't see them. Evidently they got away." As a precaution, he tightened his grip on his cousin's leg.

"But Byron?"

"Pardon me for calling him an earthworm, but earthworms know how to take care of themselves. Look straight up the trail that he left. Do you see anything?"

Harold looked intently. "No."

Pointing to a pile of stones against the barn, Miguel said, "Don't you think he's burrowed under one of them?"

Only when he felt Harold relax completely did he loosen his grip on him.

The cat had heard the squealing, but fortunately the farmer had not. Therefore, the man threw the frustrated feline onto the seat of the pickup and drove away.

Harold and Miguel went down again into the mouse house.

"Where were we when all that began?" asked Miguel.

The conversation had wandered so much that Harold could only tell the truth. "I don't know. Somewhere along the way you said something about helping the rats change their attitude. And I asked, 'But how?'"

"Oh yes," replied Miguel with a smile. "Thank you." Miguel never forgot his manners. "What we have to do is build up their self-esteem. Everybody despises them. Even mice."

"Then you're saying that everybody should say something nice to those disgusting critters." Harold was working himself into a bad, bad mood.

"See what I mean," quipped Miguel.

"But people cannot speak compliments without coloring them with veiled insults," Harold protested. "It's animal nature. For example, to praise a rat without me feeling admiration or affection would be harder than running across the yard knowing the cat was there."

"Without my feeling..." Miguel corrected instinctively. "Remember that! You make that mistake too often!" He glared at his cousin, probably revealing what he really felt about him.

"But I don't feel anything for them, unless it's loathing," Harold said. If he understood the reproof, he pretended not to.

"But how are we going to win a victory if people like you are not willing to make a concession and bend a little?" asked Miguel with a bit of sarcasm.

"People like *me!*" shouted Harold. "People like *me!* And what about you? Do you think that with your pretentious wisdom you can solve the problem?" Harold rested his chin on a paw and awaited the answer. He was actually enjoying this "civilized warfare" and was waiting to give Miguel the "coup de grace" where it hurt most.

Miguel chose to overlook the last remark and said, "Give them half a chance."

However, since Miguel pronounced "half" more like a British person would, Harold retorted with: "Give them *hawf* a *chawnce.*" That was supposed to devastate his cousin, who had never been to England.

Miguel was becoming really irritated by now. "Said like a real mouse that," he said once again in British tones.

"Yes, I *am* a mouse," replied Harold, "and I don't change my name to hide that fact." When he said that, he exaggerated his rural way of talking.

Fortunately for both, each had a sense of humor. Otherwise they would soon be throwing cakes, cups, and saucers at one another. Nevertheless, to make himself look good, Harold said, "I only did that to show how impossible it will be to do what you say."

Whether Harold was telling the truth or not, Miguel did not question. "I knew that all the time," he said as he acquiesced. "A dramatization speaks louder than the most powerful speech. The only thing that speaks louder than a good dramatization is a good slogan. We're counting on you for one."

The air had cleared. The tension had relaxed. Mistakes can prove to be like a vaccination. The patient, on being infected with a little of the disease builds up a greater resistance. They both got the point.

"Pardon me for correcting your grammar," Miguel said, "you usually don't talk incorrect." He laughed at his own deliberate mistake.

"And pardon what I just said about your name. I guess I'm just jealous. 'Bukmas' sounds human. I'd like to be treated like a man."

"Bukmas?" Miguel questioned. "Where did that come from?" And he jotted that down in his notebook.

Harold became quite uncomfortable and did not have the courage to tell him.

Chapter Four

It Takes Time to Learn Some Lessons

Cassandra Mouse woke up early. She knew that ducks also got up early and that they remembered for two or three days. Therefore, for two or three days she would do better not to appear on this side of the fence. However, what a dilemma. On the other side she exposed herself to being caught by the cat. (Of course, she did not know that temporarily there was no cat.) Also, the sound of the shotgun blast had shattered her weakened sense of security and added to her fears. However, she could not remain there, and she was hungry.

What were her options? Going home was not one. Going to the Mouse Storehouse would be the same as going home, for the other mice would see her and tell Harold. As for traveling with one of the mice, she did not like the idea. Mice gossip so. Their chitter chatter at times drove her crazy. Mice love mouselore as much as humans love folklore. Many mice are fond of the tales which date from the days when it was relatively easy (for mice) to stowaway on boats and sail the seven seas. One of them, a distant ancestor of hers–and of many, if you remember how their family trees are–made it to London. Since he was alone, he went looking for company. Suddenly, near the banks of the river Thames he happened upon a very elegant gala festival of the very best mice of London. It is rumored that then and there the people of the Bookmouse clan began to substitute the British *hawf* for the American *half*. Be that as it may, the American mouse went in, and the only thing that distinguished him from the others was his dialect. He introduced himself to them in hopes of getting acquainted.

"An American, eh? We can tell by your accent," said one a bit stuffily.

"*My* accent!" replied the voyager. "I thought *you* had the accent!" he said, trying to muster up spunk, but his remark was ill-received. Those were the days shortly after the American Revolution when, it is said, the British were more open in belittling their overseas relatives. The mouse wisely chose to let that pass. What he really wanted to do was relate his experiences at sea. But they were more interested in correcting his speech and gossiping about unfortunate London mice.

Finally, in order not to miss the benefit of the occasion, he filled his paunch with the delicacies of the feast— Dutch, French, and Italian cheeses—flavors and aromas which he had never before experienced and went to pass the night in the hollow of one of the mooring posts along the wharf. The first time you hear the account, it is fascinating. You visualize the sights and smell the aromas. However, after a hundred times...

Such were Cassandra's reveries.

When the sun showed his face more fully, the morning dampness began to be absorbed, and a multicolored butterfly appeared looking for nectar among the early-blooming flowers.

"Maybe we could travel together," thought the mouse with a certain excitement. She slipped out of her hole and through the wire mesh fence and waited among the flowers until the butterfly advanced to where she was.

She frequently despaired of even having the opportunity to greet her. As butterflies tend to do, this one darted in a zigzag fashion, at times returning to where she had just been.

Finally, she arrived to where Cassandra was waiting. When she had finished sipping, Cassandra spoke, softly at first in order not to frighten her. Nevertheless, since no butterfly has ever had a mouse wait for her, she was startled anyway.

"I'm so sorry I frightened you," Cassandra stammered. "I saw you visiting the flowers and I wanted to get acquainted with you."

The butterfly did not answer immediately. But so far so good. Butterflies almost always flit away when they are disturbed or confused. That is the complaint about them in all the Animal Kingdom. Since they are so delicate and beautiful, everyone–except birds, of course, who eat them—has dreams of being seen talking casually and at length with one of them.

"You're a mouse, aren't you?" She said after a while. Cassandra looked herself over, the full length of her body from paw to tail and said finally, "I think so." She smiled broadly, not losing hope of forming a lasting friendship with this lovely, elusive and very solitary creature.

"Do you like to travel?" asked Cassandra, as she had done in the case of the duck. Evidently, she had once again forgotten her mother's good advice.

"And if I answer that question, will you ask me another?" asked the butterfly, lighting on a leaf of the flower she had been investigating.

"Yes," said the mouse with a positive attitude. "First of all, do you?"

"Do I?"

"Do you like to travel?"

"I am a traveler. You know that. How did you know to wait for me here, if you did not know that I was a traveler?" The butterfly was beginning to show impatience and fluttered her wings very slightly.

"Now the second question," said Cassandra Mouse, who was extremely pleased with herself and hoped all the barnyard animals saw her talking to the butterfly. "Would you be interested in traveling with me?"

That was too much. The butterfly could not keep from laughing. What could have been like the melodious tingle of a glockenspiel sounded in Cassandra's tiny ear-drums like the dissonance of an orchestra whose instruments are not in tune.

"With me?" the butterfly said as she laughed again. "How could you, who can't even fly, travel with me? Or do you expect me to walk on the earth like you clumsy groundlings?"

"Oh, I could fly," Cassandra exclaimed, revealing a strange phenomenon of human nature. People think that anything they can imagine is easy to do. To prove it, she leaped upward toward the leaf where the butterfly was perched. Of course, the winged creature bore wings and accelerated out of reach. Unfortunately, because she was too heavy for the flower, the leaf snapped, and the mouse fell on her back onto the earth.

"Groundling!" shouted the butterfly scornfully as she flew away. "Aren't there enough mice for you to travel with one of them?"

Of course, we already know the reasons Cassandra did not want to travel with mice. We can only imagine her state of mind as she put herself on all fours and stretched so as not to feel stiff afterwards. Later, she would realize that she did not really want to fly with or without butterflies either. But it takes time to learn some lessons.

The sun rose higher in the sky. Whether from hunger or nervous exhaustion, Cassandra began to feel very sleepy. She dozed and nodded, bobbing her head up and down, waking up with each downswing.

When the noonday heat became unbearable, she began to look for somewhere to hide. At the same time, on hearing the duck's quacking, she knew she could not go through the fence again. Beneath the flowers was shade, and cool refreshment was to be found among the roots. There, the mouse also discovered an abundance of unsprouted seeds which had probably lain there all winter. At any rate, she ate and was refreshed. She was about to curl up for a proper nap when the sound of the farmer's truck awakened her. She had not heard it go out in the morning. Probably she had been in a deep sleep after all. That was because a small snake had crept in looking for a warm place to rest. Sensing the warmth of the mouse's body, he had wrapped himself in a circle around her, thus inducing a deep sleep in Cassandra, because of the warmth of her den.

Peeking out from between the leaves, she saw that the man had returned and was releasing three cats: a tabby, a yellowish one, and a grayish one, who appeared to be a teenager. On touching the ground, they ran about, frantically snarling and scratching at everything, for the trip over bumpy country roads had unsettled them. The farmer looked quite happy. Although it would take the cats a while to adjust to their new environment, he knew that in time his farm would be clean of rats, mice, and lizards.

Cassandra was just in time to see their first encounter. Tillie, the wife of the field mouse, was just on her way to the Mouse Storehouse when the three cats landed on the ground. She was loyal enough to the cause to not give away the location of the granary even if she had to make the supreme sacrifice. Therefore, she ran as fast as she could toward the barn. Just in time she scuddled among the rocks where Byron had buried himself the evening before. The three cats followed full speed as far as they could and then stood at bay with their strange feline bellowing.

When the man arrived, he lifted the stone, but the mouse had disappeared into the barn. There lay Byron exposed and about to inquire about the meaning of this impudent intrusion.

"Snake!" the man shouted. "Where is that hoe?" Then on looking closely, said with relief: "No, only a lowly earthworm. Too bad I don't have time to go fishing today!" And he went off about more pressing business.

Therefore, good fortune was with Byron again. Adult cats do not get interested in worms and the farmer was more interested in mice and rats than in earthworms. So once again Byron was saved. Still, he thought it better to look for an opportunity to consult again with Harold. Things were getting to be too dangerous around the farm.

Cassandra saw all of that but could not interpret it because she was too far away to hear the conversation. Of course, she did not know that Byron's hideout had been discovered. The cats disappeared behind the barn and the farmer went into the house.

Just then a floating movement caught Cassandra's attention. The butterfly had come back to see how she was doing. Cassandra did not look up because she was afraid of being disdained again and the butterfly flew away.

At length she noticed something poking up through the moist soil.

"A snake!" She remained almost paralyzed.

Little by little the animal emerged from the earth and inched steadily along like one of those spring-like toys children play with. It was an earthworm, who came out of the earth and looked at her. Her heart sank, for although she would not wish for it, this animal would have been a good traveling companion. It did not peck mice's tails. It did not gossip about other mice or worms. It did not fly. It was not beautiful, and it was not haughty. The only problem was that she did not want to be seen traveling with an earthworm.

His name was Roger, and he lost no time telling her so. "Hear you want to travel and don't have no one to do it with," he said cheerily.

"'Don't have *anyone* to travel with' is the correct way to say it," she snapped and then she was filled with wonder and curiosity. "How did you know that?"

"Everybody knows," he declared, batting his eyelashes.

"Everybody. And who exactly is everybody?" asked the mouse. She looked at the long snake-like creature with a certain disdain.

"The duck told it in the henhouse. She boasted that she wanted to fool you so she could make you her mascot or pet, as men say." It gave Roger great pleasure to know something so humiliating about another animal. "I bet you thought you were going to ride all over the world on duckie's back didn't you?" He laughed raucously.

"Not exactly," said Mrs. Mouse, and she shared her mother's advice about friends at first sight. Still it was hard to know that she was being made a laughingstock. "But you don't dare go near the henhouse, so how did you know?"

"Well as I said, everybody's talking about you. You probably know that people like to compare worms with snakes. Really worms and snakes have no dealings at all with one another. They don't love each other and they don't hate one another either. They never live together. If a worm is about to enter a hole and smells that snakes are there or have been there, he keeps going. And snakes are the same way. If we meet on a trail, we nod politely to each other and one takes to the right side of the road and the other takes the opposite. The same way humans do when they drive their cars and buggies on the road."

As his comment was becoming quite long, the mouse interrupted. She remembered hearing that worms talk according to the length of their body. This one, although obviously young–too young to realize that a lady mouse could not travel with a gentleman worm–was very long.

"But what does your very long tale have to do with

how my story got out of the henhouse?"

"What a minute, Lady, what do you mean my very long tail. It's not my fault if I'm tall for my age!" He found her words insulting.

"I'm so sorry I hurt your feelings," Cassandra said and laughed. "You see, a tale is also a story. However, your tail is the lower part of your body. I have a tail too." She stopped when she realized that her explanation was competing with the worm's tale for length.

"I was about to tell you how your story got out of the henhouse, but you rudely interrupted my thoughts. You know how snakes like to come out and warm themselves in the morning sun?" he continued.

"Oh no!" exclaimed the exasperated mouse, fearing that Roger would continue.

"Don't get impatient," said Roger with a chuckle. "Don't get impatient! Well, anyway, as I was saying, this morning I came out of my hole to stretch and warm up when I came upon this young snake basking himself in the sun. I could see he was too young to know if he should like me or despise me, so I eased up to him. We started talking all friendly like when he told me his tale.

'I am lost from my parents,' he told me. 'The night before, my parents ventured into the henhouse to eat eggs and they took me with them to teach me. Then we heard the commotion. Duck was fit to be tied because some mouse had gotten away, and when she saw us, she attacked with fury. Although we managed to escape, we were separated and I managed to hide under some piled up stones alongside that fence there. I was cold but, on entering, I sensed warmth. There, curled up tight as an angry man's fist was a mouse. I imagine it was the same one the duck was hunting. Anyway I wrapped myself in a circle around her, and we both slept soundly. Since I woke up first, I crawled off. She never knew when I came in and when I went out.'"

On hearing that, Mrs. Mouse shuttered and realized that what she had thought to be a dream had been in fact reality. Why has she left home in the first place? What would respectable mice think of her spending the night in a hole with a young snake and then of a young worm's inviting himself to travel with her? Leaving home to travel was not such a good idea after all!

"Please don't tell me more," pleaded the mouse. "I have a delicate heart. My mother told me that mice have passed away just at the thought of danger."

"Okay, okay, but do we travel together or not?"

Cassandra thought, *I have spoken a lot without thinking lately. Oh, let these words count.*

A moment or two passed without her speaking. The earthworm waited. Finally she said, "I'm flattered that you should consider me as a traveling companion, but I'm afraid that would be quite impossible. You see I am a woman and you are..."

"A worm?" interrupted Roger.

"Well, that's not exactly what I had in mind," she con-

•39•

tinued. "Were you a worm, a butterfly, or a mouse, you are a man."

"Don't insult me. I am not a man, I am a worm. Who could criticize a mouse and a worm for traveling together?" he asked, becoming quite stubborn. He was a cousin of Byron on his father's side, one who would probably come to no good end.

"You know what I mean," said Mrs. Mouse with a tone of finality.

"Sure I do," replied the worm. "I guess I would have been surprised if you would have answered any other way."

"Well, Roger," Mrs. Mouse replied, "I must be going." She got up, shook off the chaff from the seeds, licked her paws and arranged her face with her moistened hands.

"Oh yeah, I forgot to tell you. Your cousin Miguel Bookmouse is telling all the mice that if they see you to tell you to go home right away. Something big is about to happen."

Just then a lonely fly came up. "The butterfly told me that you were looking for a traveling companion. Here I am. The most ideal. You won't have to fly to keep up with me. I'll just stick to your hide. The dirtier the better."

"That does it!" squeaked Cassandra.

With Roger laughing as heartily as he could, Cassandra ran away. She crossed the dried turf with the fly chasing close upon her heels. Just in time did she enter the front porch of her house and pass through the tunnel to the front door. By the time the fly found the opening, the mouse was in her house. Fortunately for her the cats had not appeared.

Chapter Five

The World is a Dangerous Place

On entering the house, Cassandra noted that Harold had "replanted" the branch which represented the clan of the Bookmouses. What could possibly have overcome her husband? She felt more apprehensive because of the warning that something big was about to happen bolstered by the gunshot she had heard the day before.

The lamp was on, but the overhead light, off. That cast a soft glow over the room, reminding her of how much she enjoyed being at home. The fly's frenzied buzzing also made her very grateful to be inside.

"Harold. Harold," she called. "I'm back." She said that as if she had only stepped out momentarily to visit the Mouse Storehouse.

Harold came out slowly, torn between two emotions. On the one hand, the old Harold wanted to scold her for being out all night. On the other hand, the reformed Harold commanded him to apologize for the way he had ignored her. Caught between the two, he shifted from one foot (for they had adopted the human custom of walking upright when at home) to the other, saying nothing.

Cassandra was very sentimental. When Timmy was born, she had laid him in his leaf-lined cradle and sung the following verse:

> *To be born in a hole in the ground*
> *Is the greatest joy of all.*
> *Cavern life underground*
> *Is what should befall*
> *A mouse,*
> *A mouse.*
> *Being born in a cavern underground*
> *Is the joy that should befall a mouse.*
> *An experience that even humans should share.*

Baby Timmy fell asleep against the background of her clear soprano voice.

"Oh, Harold," she would say dreamily, "isn't he the most beautiful baby in the whole of Mousedom?"

Of course Harold thought so. After all, Timmy was his first and only son. "Sorry, Son," he thought, "Timothy Mouse is what you will be for life, and not 'Bukmas.'"

"Oh, Harold," Cassandra pleaded, "let's promise each other to keep him ever secure here. We won't raise our voices at each other or at him. We'll raise him in perfect peace and keep the confusion of the outside world outside, where it belongs. What do you say Harold? Do you promise? Please? Please."

Harold had become uncomfortable because he knew it was impossible to shut out completely the uproar of the outside world. Therefore, he did not answer right away.

"Harold, why don't you answer me? You don't want our son to grow up to be like a rat, do you?"

For some reason that remark had intimidated and irritated him. What power did he have to make his son grow up to be like a mouse and not to be like a rat? He felt his wife was throwing a very heavy burden upon him. The sparks of irritation were already beginning to kindle. If he had expressed his frustrations at that moment he might not have been so completely immersed in his own feelings the day Byron entered as an unexpected visitor.

Timmy grew by leaps and bounds and soon was getting into everything, as toddlers will do. Harold was not prepared for the demands of fatherhood and grew increasingly more tense and moody. Cassandra, in turn, sensing that Harold's inconsistency could rub off on Timothy somehow, became more and more demanding.

As Timothy grew from day to day, he became everything but docile and calm. He was a hyper-active child who turned everything inside out and upside down. Their idyllic mousehole—cavern underground as Cassandra had sung—was becoming too small. However, it was impossible to let him go outside to play. Other mice children had done that and had not come back. But Cassandra could not seem to understand that. Apparently, she expected Harold to put an end to the war outside and establish harmony in their home.

Thus, the tension between them kept building up to a crescendo until Cassandra decided to travel for a while in order to cool off a little.

Harold spoke at last. "I'm glad you came back. If you hadn't, I might have married a young rat by mistake."

They both laughed. Harold's comment showed that the bond between them had not been broken. They still thought alike.

"Timothy's asleep. Shush. Don't wake him up. He nearly drove me crazy. Sit down. I'll make tea."

While Harold was brewing the tea, Cassandra crept in to look at her little boy. The experiences of the past twenty-four hours had given her a new perspective. Together, they had to do something to better regulate the child's upbringing before the situation caused another separation.

Harold came with tea and biscuits. They sat side-by-side on the sofa and Cassandra related with worm-like detail what had happened. Harold became indignant when he heard about the presumptuous duck. He flinched when she mentioned the young snake curled up in a circle around her. He reproached the haughty butterfly for not realizing what a privilege it would have been to travel with Cassandra.

"Did you tell her you can make crochet butterflies more beautiful than she? Of all the nerve!"

"Now, Harold," Cassandra quieted him. "I realize now that I don't really want to go around with arrogant people. Don't feel bad for me."

"But can you imagine that duck telling everybody that she meant to fool you in order to capture you as a pet?" Harold could no longer drink his tea or eat his biscuits.

"Harold, what a close call. I could be in the henhouse now with a chain around one of my feet and the hens pecking me on the tail." She put one paw over her heart in an expression of great relief.

Harold took her paw and caressed it. "I'm so glad you escaped," he said. "But the snake. Was he one of those that eat...?"

"Mice?" Cassandra completed his thought. "I'm sure he was, but he was still as small as a worm and only wanted to get warm."

"Still, that was a close call. What if his parents had found him! I bet he'll get a bawling out when he tells them what happened," Harold looked serious and very sad.

Then she told him about the fresh young worm and how she refused to travel with him because a lady and a gentleman cannot travel together. "It doesn't matter that he is a worm and I, a mouse. It's a matter of principle. Some things just are not done," she said. "I wouldn't have said that a week ago. Of course, I hadn't run away from home a week ago either."

"You know," mused Harold, "I'm beginning to understand that there are principles which are greater even than inherent differences." He sipped his tea and remained silent for a moment.

Cassandra interrupted the silence. "And then that disgusting fly. And to think that the butterfly sent him. That only shows that when you do one thing wrong, everything can come out wrong. He said that I wouldn't have to fly. I could carry him on my back and the dirtier I was the better. Harold, the next time I go crazy like that, block the door. The world is a dangerous place."

Since it is always dark underground without windows, they did not know what time it was. A glance at the clock revealed that they had been at their conversation about three hours. Miraculously, the baby had not awakened.

"Let me make seed porridge with raisins for supper," said Cassandra. "Thank you, Harold for listening to my adventure. I feel as if we never quarreled."

"I'm sorry I shut you out, Cassandra," said Harold. That is what he had wanted to say when he was caught between the two Harolds. And now he felt unburdened, having learned how important it was for a husband to listen to his wife.

Just then, Byron tapped on the door. The fly's buzzing became more furious because he wanted to come in too. Cassandra parted the curtains and called to Harold, who came running. He was relieved to know that his friend had not been damaged by the gunshot.

"Harold," Cassandra said, "tell him to come in through

---

the old way so that the fly won't come in with him."

If they had spoken a foreign language, Harold could have told him in that tongue and the fly would not have been able to decipher. However, they only had the common language which all animals use, by means of which they understand human speech as well. So, he tried something innovative.

"Byron," he said a little above a whisper, "Sorry but we can't open the door." And he held up a sign that said W B-4 U.

"Understand?" he asked, hopefully.

"Sure," said the visitor. But the truth was that he did not and he went away very sad. "'W B-4 U.' 'Double U before you.' Could that be it? Double U. Go out the front way and make a U-turn. Then another U-turn should take me just about to the place where I burrowed into the mice's den."

The fly, who did not understand, was delighted at the worm's being turned away and kept on buzzing with vicious defiance.

Byron crawled out of the tunnel and veered to the left in order to deceive the pesky fly. Then he crawled behind the opening over the passageway and made his double U-turn. The earth was still soft where Harold had filled in the worm's entrance. Harold and Cassandra did not help, though they very much wanted to see him, because Byron's method was to move the dirt backwards inside-out. That way the cozy mouse house would not fill up with debris.

At last Byron's head peeked through. His glasses almost fell off. "They keep telling me to invest in contact lenses," he said laughing as he eased his way into the living room.

"Oh, Byron," Cassandra squealed. "We're so glad you came back!"

"Thank you, Cassandra," he said, a little uncomfortably. He was thinking about Harold's farewell remark, "It wasn't your fault. It wasn't anybody's, really." He was not sure that he was in agreement. Harold and he had been so engrossed in conversation yesterday when Cassandra said she was going to the market that nobody had heard her. She said she had repeated three times that she was going and nobody had responded. Byron had been the first to hear, but it was almost more than he could do to stop Harold's commentary. He was expounding on the way to help animals cope with a feeling of rejection. Inferiority complexes were common among animals, especially rats and flies.

Cassandra had gone out and come back as many as seven times to see if anyone would pay her attention, even the teeniest little bit of attention. When Byron had succeeded in shaking Harold loose from his dissertation, Cassandra was running up the tunnel. On hearing Harold's voice, with tear-filled eyes she had screamed, "I am leaving because you *never* listen to me! You are more interested in any *worm* that crawls in without invitation than in your *own wife!*"

Throughout it all, Timmy ran pointlessly about, plowing into everything.

Harold was becoming more and more impatient. "Cassandra, you come back here this minute. I command you!" The tremble in his voice gave lie to his claims to great authority.

She laughed scornfully. "I'm going to travel first. I need to get to know who *I* am. Only then will I return. And when I get back, I better find the hole that w_ _ _," even though she was angry she couldn't say it, "the hole that, that *trespasser* made plastered and bricked over."

Byron had crawled up the entranceway almost immediately.

The question when he returned was, in fact, who should apologize and to whom? Byron felt he should, since he had been out of place. Perhaps it would be easier for a lowly earthworm to admit he had made a mistake than for a mouse.

Nevertheless, Cassandra's spoke first. "Oh, Byron, will you ever forgive me for calling you a worm?" She patted him gently on his uplifted head.

"Well, Cassandra, after all, that's what I am."

She laughed. "Don't be silly, Byron. You know what I mean!"

Since some comments are better left unanswered, Byron simply acquiesced with a pleasant beam.

"Good, good, so we're all sorry," exclaimed Harold

with a generous air.

"But I've got nothing to be sorry about," said Cassandra rather perturbed. "I had to go out and come in seven times before I could get anybody's attention." Her voice became increasingly shriller. At that, Timothy woke up and began calling for attention. Harold lifted his arms in a gesture of despair and helplessness. Byron began looking longingly at the tunnel he had burrowed into the house. In that instant, a loud banging was heard on the front door.

Chapter Six
Illegal Underground Activity

It was Miguel Bookmouse. He had gotten rid of the fly by telling him that if he came in, he would have to take a bath. As you remember, Miguel was an investigator and knew a lot about animals, and he knew that a fly with wet wings could not fly. Still, he entered through as narrow an opening in the door as possible, just in case the insect returned. What met his eye was the confusion we just saw. He came in time to calm them down or, at least, to turn their minds to other subjects. So that kept them from devouring one another.

He addressed Byron first. "You, here?"

"Yes," he answered positively. "I became aware of the danger facing the mouse and rat population of the barn-yard and I came to see if I could help out somehow."

Prudently he had mentioned mice before rats since he was talking to mice. To rats, he would diplomatical-ly have had to say "rat and mouse" population. But in a meeting at which both mice and rats were present, what would be the safest thing to say. "Rodents?" He did not know if "rodent" was an offensive word or not. At any rate, mice do not like to be classified with rats. It would take a skillful speaker to address a combined group and not offend someone.

"I see," replied Miguel, rather coolly.

Byron saw that his first challenge would be to win, not the rats' confidence, but Miguel's.

Harold suggested that they sit down. Since worms do not coil up like snakes and can form the figure "S," they can sit down on chairs, just as other animals do. A snake would probably have to coil around the basket in the corner. But if a snake came in, the mice would run out. Therefore, he could coil around any piece of furniture he chose.

Cassandra went to bring Timmy and then to bring the seed cakes and tea. On noticing that Byron did not help himself to the cakes, she asked "What do you people eat?"

Byron felt warm inside. "Don't worry yourself about anything, Cassandra. I'll just drink a little tea."

Cassandra wanted her guests to feel comfortable. "It's chamomile. Do you drink chamomile?" she asked solicitously.

"Chamomile is fine," Byron responded.

"But do you like it?"

"I don't know," replied Byron. "That's why am going to try it. To find out." He curled his long body in such a way that he could hover over the cup on the coffee table and absorb the steamy liquid.

Cassandra, quicker than a flash, snatched the cup away. Harold was about to become alarmed. However, Cassandra asked, "What would you really enjoy, Byron? Chamomile might have something—some hidden ingredient—that does you harm."

Byron thought a moment. "Do you have anything "earthy" or "rooty" to make a brew?" He looked around. He noticed that tiny roots were entering the roof of the cavern. Harold had commented that Cassandra liked to cut them close like a ceiling cover to complement the paper and walls. In wet weather moisture got trapped there and if no one touched the ceiling, the water stayed. It was a built-in vaporizing system which was part of Cassandra's plan to keep the home environment clean so Timothy would not have to go out of the house. Nevertheless, some rootlets were longer than others, and Cassandra skillfully with the kitchen shears snipped off enough to make a nice pot of tea. Fortunately, it had not rained recently.

While the tea was brewing, Miguel, Byron, and Harold commented on Timothy's growth. He would soon be three months old, almost a teenager. His cousin Lemuel was already a big boy when he had that close call. Since mice grow up so fast, there's no definite adolescent stage. A young mouse can pass from child to teenager in a matter of seconds, and that is just exactly what happened with Timothy. When Cassandra returned from the kitchen with Byron's tea she saw a change in her baby which was so noticeable that she almost dropped the tray.

No longer restless, nor seemingly mindless, he was actually sitting beside Byron and paying attention to the conversation.

Miguel took the lead. "The situation has become more serious than it was before. The farmer got rid of the incompetent cat and has brought three more. And the youngest one–the gray one–will wipe us out due to his nervous energy if not his skill. He just caught our cousin's son, Lemuel."

Cassandra let out a little shriek which was enough to let the cat know where they lived.

"Shh," he warned, "I think he suspects there's illegal underground activity going on around here." He paused to let the effect of his humor soak in. He felt good to know he could laugh even in the face of crises. However, his listeners were too overwhelmed with fear to see anything funny.

Miguel continued. "That young one saw me approaching so I didn't come straight in. Instead I went through the wire fence and hid among the herbs that grow there. Since he was too big to fit through the mesh, he had to find a place where he could jump over. Here his youth was my advantage. Perfect timing and his lack of experience are what saved me. When he was leaping for the top rail of the fence I ran forward along the fence, and then, like a fox, I ran back across my own tracks and leaped through the wire mesh and hid among the piled-up rocks."

"Exactly where I spent the night," Cassandra interrupted. "We'll have to build a monument there when the war is over." Then, over Miguel's protest because he wanted to continue with his presentation, she went on to relate about the beautiful butterfly, the earthworm and the fly.

"Earthworm?" Byron asked.

"Yes," said Cassandra, becoming indignant all over again. "His name is Roger and he came looking for me because he heard I was looking for a traveling companion."

"He always was fresh," snapped Byron. "His parents can't discipline him even with stories about fishhooks and runaway plows."

"You know him then?"

"Yes, he's my father's brother's son."

"Anyway," interrupted Miguel. "Whether because he hunts by smell or by sight, I lost that varmint and ran straight here when I heard the hens and the ducks inquiring who he was, where he had come from, and what he was doing there. How much food do you have stored up here? How long can you remain inside without going out?"

Harold thought deeply. "Two weeks perhaps."

"Good," Miguel replied. "Maybe the problem can be solved within two weeks. But whatever you do, don't let

Timothy outside. He's too new to the world. And his new-found maturity—well time will tell just how far it goes. But, at any rate, don't let him go outside. After the victory we'll sit out under the stars and enjoy nature like we haven't been able to do in a mouse's age."

All had become very solemn and thoughtful, a bit dejected.

Byron spoke first. "With that young cat, I'm at risk too because the young ones take us for strings and like to play with us. At least I can travel underground if it's necessary to deliver a message." It was then that the humor of Miguel's comment about underground activity hit him, and he began to laugh heartily. "Underground activity. Underground activity. Underground activity," he kept saying over and over again almost in a whisper.

When Miguel tried to continue, Byron's laughter once again interrupted him. It made Miguel feel good to know that someone else could appreciate his thoughts. When at last he was able to go on, he added, "Now where were we? Oh, yes, the challenge of persuading the rats to change their attitude. Attitude? Is that the word we agreed on, Harold?"

Harold nodded in consent. "There are still a lot of them although their numbers are decreasing," Miguel said, "and I hear they're planning an invasion of the farmhouse itself! When rats do that men call exterminators, and I tell you, no decent creatures survive that experience."

"But how can we help the rats change or improve their attitude?" Cassandra cried out at last.

"Building up their self-esteem so that they don't feel the need to defy an enemy who is much, much, much more powerful. Teaching them—or rather—encouraging them to be clean, to store up provisions. Like we have done—"

"But we better not make comparisons between them and us," Harold interrupted, "because they'll just riot, that's all."

"Why should that be?" Cassandra complained. "We mice have certainly accomplished more than other people around the barn yard, except of course the ants."

"But people don't like to hear that others have accomplished more than they have. It tends to make them angry," Harold explained.

"Then they should humble themselves and accept that they need to improve," Cassandra declared with finality, as if the conversation were closed. She was becoming nervous and irritated, and Harold was afraid she might run out of the house again—and disappear for good.

The tea had been drunk. The seed cakes had been consumed. For all appearances the conversation would go on for hours. Therefore, Harold asked Cassandra to prepare more food and beverages, for them and for Byron.

When she had entered the kitchen, Harold commented: "You see how difficult—if not to say impossible—our task is. First you and I almost came to blows just talking about how to build others up. Now Cassandra is fit to be tied. I'm not hungry. I just wanted to get her busy doing something so as to take her mind off the rats. Miguel, it's just not animal nature to look for the good in others. I tell you, in the actual meeting, someone is going to put his foot in his mouth, and the rats are going to declare war on us."

Miguel looked really worried now. He knew Harold was making a strong point. "And Byron, what do you think?" His condescension was beginning to disappear, and you could almost imagine a certain warmth for the worm was beginning to kindle in his mind.

"We'd better figure out what to say in order to not upset the uh...is it safe to use the word 'rats'?" Byron felt disconcerted.

"I think so," Miguel answered. "Harold?"

"The word's in the dictionary," Harold answered. "We are mice. 'MOUSE' (plural, mice) is in the dictionary. Also 'earthworm.'" He was beginning to lose confidence once again. "Byron, on speaking to a group of people of your biological order, what word should we use?"

Now it was Byron's turn to be unsure. "What we don't like is the term 'lowly' as in 'lowly earthworm,'" he said after thinking it over a moment. "It would be acceptable to say 'dear' or 'fellow earthworms.' Well, perhaps not 'fellow' because that implies that the speaker is an earthworm too. But if he's not, the earthworm community is likely to be offended. Better 'Dear Earthworms!'" He was becoming comfortable in his discourse, which was becoming worm-like in length, and Miguel finally had to cut him off.

"Byron," he said bristling with irritation, "Save the diatribe for peace times. The question was, Is earthworm an acceptable expression, or would it offend a group of your people?"

Byron throbbed at Miguel's condescension and answered, "Earthworm can be used without offending." He was going to add a postlude about lowly earthworm, but he thought better about it.

Chapter Seven
We Face a Common Danger

The next day Miguel summoned a meeting of the more responsible mice of the community. Because of Byron, it was diplomatically necessary to invite a few worms also. And since the duck had swallowed a frog, a number of frog delegates were also included. The only safe place for all was at the far end of the orchard. The cats had not yet learned to venture there. As for the farmer, he only entered during certain hours, according to a strict schedule, and the children were forbidden to play there.

It was a sunny morning when about twenty-five delegates assembled themselves at the foot of an apple tree in full bloom. Miguel, always well-organized, had prepared a written agenda, neatly printed in long-hand, his special calligraphy. He had taken care to cut the paper with tiny scissors in the form of sheets instead of using shreds of paper as mice generally do. He also calculated that if the sheets were neatly cut, the worms might be dissuaded from using them to make compost. It was said among the animals that frogs do not read. However, in order to not offend them, Miguel had prepared agendas for the frogs, as well. The purpose of the convention was to convince the united animals of their common danger and solicit their help. Too, he had thought about practice sessions, some pretending to be rats, so that they could train themselves to reason with their energetic neighbors.

A festive mood reigned in spite of everything. They spoke in the tongue of men and beasts. There were seed cakes and chamomile tea for the mice, rootbrew for the earthworms and honey to attract flies, to please the frogs.

The frogs entertained first with their strange music. Human sometimes say it is soothing, against a background of crickets, on a summer evening. Mice and worms listen at times also, but generally only when there is nothing better to do. However, today the principal theme was, "Be open-minded when dealing with others."

Unfortunately, Roger was present although he had not been invited. His presence made Cassandra very uncomfortable and Byron, very angry.

"Come back already? What kind of trip was that?" he asked Cassandra loud enough for the other mice to hear, and chuckled maliciously.

Cassandra and Harold held their peace.

Miguel, hoping to avoid an embarrassing scene, clapped his hands together to call the meeting to order, but since mouse paws are made to run silently nobody heard or paid attention.

"We heard about your trip, Cassandra," said Tillie. "The fly told us you were sending out messages in hopes of finding a traveling companion." The titter of mouse laughter could be heard as an accompaniment to the frogs' bass line.

Cassandra felt the blood rush to her face. When a mouse blushes, she looks like a chipmunk, only darker. She almost wished the cat would come. She closed her eyes and, to her further consternation, heard a familiar buzz. True, all flies make a buzzing noise, and most people cannot distinguish between one and another. But when you have been pursued by an impetuous, disrespectful fly, you recognize his voice among a thousand others.

"Why didn't you want to travel with Roger, Cassandra?" asked another mouse. "Was it because he's a lowly earthworm?"

Roger stood up like a cobra and protested. "Forget that expression, people! There is no such thing as a lowly earthworm." Roger, when he was irritated, was even more unpleasant than when he was simply being rambunctious. When he was insulting, he only wanted to embarrass you. But when he was provoked, he was a formidable enemy.

Roger's outburst had interrupted even the frog's serenade. Nothing was heard except the sound of the flying insect, buzzing, buzzing, buzzing along, to the humiliation of Cassandra. No one knew his name or how he knew about the meeting. Really, nobody had to tell a fly about a secret meeting.

Early every morning the farmer inspected his trees for signs of insects or disease. He raked the soil, at times spread fertilizer and watered it, if necessary. The spiders knew that he would clear away their cobwebs, but that didn't matter. Rapidly they build more because they knew they could trap enough insects to live on before the farmer swept away their house the following day.

Cassandra still had her eyes closed. The buzzing drew nearer and louder.

"Tell them how you wanted to travel with me, but I wouldn't let you!" the fly taunted.

"That's a lie!" Harold shouted.

"Silence," Miguel said, very solemnly.

Cassandra wanted to cry. *When you make one mistake in judgment sometimes you have to keep paying for it*, she thought.

The fly, now almost frantic with excitement, zoomed down to hit Cassandra on the head, coming dangerously close to the spiderweb in the process. He cut his descent and threw on the brakes, forcing his body backwards, all the while laughing insanely. It was such a spectacle that even the mice who had been ridiculing Cassandra begin to feel sorry for her. For the moment that is, because mice do love to gossip.

Suddenly there was complete silence. A frog had done his job, and since other flies had been attracted to the honey, the other frogs also ate.

And Roger had disappeared.

The frogs were sitting upon a stone which was protruding from the earth. The earthworms were in a disorganized fashion under the shadow of a nearby stone. The mice had formed a "nest"—they would say "a sitting area"—among the grass at the foot of the tree. Miguel was in the middle. Once again, he touched his paws together and, this time, because they all saw him do it, all became silent.

"Friends," he said simply, without trying to group them into classes. "We are here because we face a common danger."

"What is it?" asked the leader of the frogs, an elderly man with a neatly trimmed beard.

"The rats," replied Miguel.

The frogs looked at him in disbelief. They were not even sure they knew what a rat was.

"Rats are something like me," he said, truly hurt to hear himself talking like that. "Like us," he said making a sweeping gesture with his hand at the company of fourteen mice (seven couples) which was lounging in the grass. "Only they are larger."

Without looking, he could feel the burning indignation of his kinsman. He preferred to concentrate on the fixed, blank stares of the three frogs who had come to the meeting rather than look at the mice.

"But what does that have to do with us?" asked another frog.

"The duck mistook me for a frog and ate a frog instead," Cassandra said. She had raised her hand, but commented without being recognized by the chair.

"Order, please," said Miguel firmly.

A breeze was beginning to stir and every once in a while, a piece of cut, dried grass flew idly by. It was a perfectly relaxing setting, a beautiful day.

Miguel tried to explain, in terms that might win the frogs' sympathy, how the rats' rebellious conduct was jeopardizing the well-being of all the barnyard animals. He did not have to address the worms because, with the exception of Byron who almost considered himself a mouse, all the others had burrowed into the soft, damp earth beneath the stone where they had stretched out at first, and were now fast asleep.

"That unfortunate froglet was my son," said the elderly frog. "We miss him, of course, but we frogs are like the worms in that we do not grieve when our loved one comes to a tragic end. I presume that mice do."

"Yes," replied Cassandra, once again without asking for permission. "My little cousin was caught by the man's young gray—and might I add—savage cat just yesterday."

Miguel was beginning to become impatient once again, and Harold began tugging at Cassandra's arm. She stopped talking.

The frogs could not see how they were involved, and the mice were becoming impatient to hear just what they

could do. The truth was that Miguel was hoping to per-
suade the frogs to hop around the barnyard the night
of the meeting with all the rats in order to distract the
cats. If they got killed, it would be a sacrifice for a wor-
thy cause. Besides, they themselves say they feel nothing
when a comrade falls. However, he was counting on the
assistance of hundreds of frogs. What he did not know
is that there are not even hundreds of frogs in the immediate vicinity. Obviously, the mice would have to think of
something else. Therefore, he courteously thanked the
aquatic friends for their time and bade them farewell.
However, they did not hop away before eating another
dozen or so flies.

The mice continued. Their future looked bleak. Byron
crawled over to where the mice were sitting, but some of
them got up and moved to another place. There is neither
enmity nor friendship between mice and worms. They
do not love each other, but neither do they fight against
each other. However, mice know that some worms work
in compost heaps where there is a lot of manure.

Cassandra knew why they had moved because she
had heard them muttering. *But Byron has never worked
in one of "those places,"* she thought. In fact, there was
one of "those places" in the corner of the orchard. "The
only worms who work in compost heaps are those who
have been put there by men," she said.

The mice who had separated themselves from the
group did not look at her, whether from shame or indig-

nation, she did not know. However, Cassandra continued with her usual impulsiveness. "Be reasonable!"

Nevertheless, the field mouse Tillie almost screamed, "But once there, do they like it?"

Cassandra was speechless. She looked at Byron, who dropped his head.

"Are they there only because men put them there, or do they like to work among garbage and manure?"

Miguel did not wait for an answer. It was already noon, and the sun was becoming hotter. Also, it would probably be dangerous to prolong the meeting much longer. In the cooler part of the evening, the farmer walked about and perhaps his children and cats with him.

"Brothers," he began imploringly, for there were only mice present with the exception of Byron, who sympathized completely with their cause. "Let us not forget the purpose of our being here and the eminent danger."

The sun was now directly overhead and cast floral shadows in a circle around the tree, whose extensive roots were their amphitheater.

"How shall we present ourselves to the rats? Who ventures to propose something? Please understand that we are wasting valuable time with personal and, permit me to say, petty issues."

However, two hours is a long while for mice to be still. When they took the final count, only Miguel, Harold, Cassandra, Tillie and her husband Rudolf—an obstinate senior citizen who was anxious to set things straight—

and, of course, Byron were willing to go and reason with the rats.

Miguel spoke with the head honcho, Arnold (who incidentally was the father of Stacey, the young rat whose life had been accidentally saved by Cassandra's cousin Lemuel), and the assembly was scheduled for eight o'clock the following evening.

Chapter Eight
Build Up Their Self-Respect

The rats themselves agreed to distract the cats. For them it would be great entertainment. If they succeeded in making these cats look bad, maybe the farmer would cart them away as he had done with the other cat. A good strategy was necessary because the cats had taken to sleeping in the barn. But the barn was the best place to have the meeting since there were at least thirty-five rats. There had been seventy, but the cats had dragged a few off, and the others had entered into mysterious-looking boxes and not been seen again. This fact had them disconcerted because, in spite of the fact that the farmer no longer used the traps with cheese, more of their brothers were disappearing than ever.

As Miguel had asked him to do, Harold had prepared slogans which would be unfurled on a banner behind the small, makeshift platform they had hastily erected in a clearing among the haystacks. Since the hay was placed in tiers, forming a stairway for delegates to go up to the top, the rats seated themselves in as orderly a fashion as humans do at their ballgames.

At 7:30, three robust young rats had begun their work of cutting a caper with the cats. One of them was a pack rat who had recently joined the community and he had collected three rubber balls. He pushed one across the floor and straight through the door which was always left ajar so the cats could go out during the night. The young cat immediately pursued it and the other two followed him, somewhat reluctantly.

Once they had them outside, another rat pushed another ball. The frisky cat chased it while the bigger ones sat and looked. Then suddenly the third rat pushed the third ball. There was thus one ball for each cat. Two of them collided chasing their balls, which made them sit still in confusion. The rats watched cautiously from under cover to see what the cats would do next. Two of the cats curled up, one around the other and went to sleep. The young one kept amusing himself for a while. At regular intervals, a ball was sent his way from different directions.

Meanwhile the meeting began at eight o'clock sharp. Miguel gave the introductory address. In it he mentioned facts which were familiar to all: the disappearance of about a half of the rat community and the loss of countless young, inexperienced mice.

The rats nodded in approval. So far, so good. Then Miguel introduced Harold, who had prepared three slogans to stimulate the rats to action. Harold had not told Miguel exactly what he was thinking about doing. He carefully pinned up a banner which was folded lengthwise through the middle so that it could not be read until he unfolded it. It said:

RATS, RAID THE FARMHOUSE!

When Miguel saw it, he became weak in the knees. He wondered why he had not debated the subject with his cousin in private knowing how capricious he was.

Nevertheless, Harold was both astute and intelligent. He understood human nature. If they had told the assembled rats, "Don't go to the farmhouse," or "Don't you dare enter Farmer Felix's house," the entire assembly would have screamed, "Nobody's going to tell us what to do!" and they would have gone directly over there.

At the same time, that was not exactly the message that the rats were expecting. For that reason, it took them a few seconds to react.

"Raid the farmhouse?" one asked. "What kind of advice is that? We expected a lot of propaganda about building storehouses like the mice, and we were prepared to refute you."

Harold looked up and saw that Roger, the worm was among the rats, sitting in S-formation on one of the upper tiers. He had thought to betray the mice, but so far he had been foiled. The rats did not even seem to notice his presence in spite of how different he was. Rats of all ages, men, women, and children were present. Rats, like mice, can only be still for about two hours so Miguel knew that the meeting had to progress. For that reason, he was about to take over when another delegate who was sitting in the middle of the bleachers screamed out, "This is nothing but mouse propaganda to get us in trouble!"

Thereupon, the rats begin to call out at the top of their voices until one of the young rats who stood guard at the door rushed to warn them that they might be heard. "Shh," he cautioned. "The cats are piled up one on top of another, sound asleep."

The rats stopped their clamor. By then, the one who had made the outcry had reached the platform. He raised his arms high to quieten down the group and bowed, which only served to evoke more outcries. With difficulty he restored order again.

"Brothers and friends," he said, for they considered the mice their equals. "Do not be alarmed by what you read on the poster, for they are mere words. I am sure that if our friend, Mr. Mouse, were given the opportunity to present his case he would succeed in convincing us that the very opposite is true, that we do not need to go and that it would be very dangerous for us to go near the house."

The rats applauded wildly, and Miguel looked at Harold in disbelief.

"Give us more information," called someone who was sitting on the front row.

"I'll give it," called a pert young adult rat whose accent

indicated that he had not grown up on that farm.

Many wondered where he was from and, for that reason, missed the import of his speech. Actually, he was a former university student from out East. He was dressed in navy blue trousers, a white shirt with blue pin stripes, a navy blue bow tie with polka dots, and cordovan loafers. His large frame glasses made him look quite scholarly. Since it was cool that evening, he also wore a khaki-colored trench coat.

His story was that he had hidden in the dormitory room of two young geniuses at one of those upscale universities during the entire four years of their undergraduate studies. Although the young men were studious, they were also pack rats. So it had been very easy for the small animal to stow away under piles of clothes and clutter on the floor of the room. He ate the crumbs which fell from the desks. (The university's administration would even pay money to keep that story out of the tabloid press.) At any rate, by listening as the collegians debated their theories, the rat acquired the equivalent of a university education.

From his undergraduate hosts he had learned about something which humans called "civil rights." So after leaving the university, he traveled west to pioneer in the field of "pack rights."

Having commanded the attention of the congress, he commenced his speech, "The farmer knows we live here, but it's as if he expected us to be here. I know that stories which men teach their children have rats and mice in them and that they even picture us in a very endearing way."

The only illumination they had was the light which filtered in from the barnyard, yet they could see him well enough, for these small animals can see in the dark. They observed that he was an impressive figure indeed, a hope, perhaps for the inhabitants of the barn.

"Apparently, what irritated the man were our overly impertinent antics. For example, the day he took the incapable cat away was the day the youngsters were evidently playing soccer on the lawn, apparently trying to use the cat as the ball. By the way whose children are they?"

There ensued a silence. Nobody wanted to answer.

"See there!" the young diplomat continued. "How many times do we have to exhort you to discipline your children?"

The further silence was proof of their shame. Miguel and all the mouse delegation understood what was happening. If one of them had broached such a sensitive subject, even delicately, that would surely have provoked a riot. However, because of his airs—different but not too different, and certainly not haughty—the rats accepted him as their hero and spokesman.

Miguel would have liked to try to address the assembly in an effort to conciliate them. He believed in exhortation by means of complimentary remarks to build up the rats' self-respect. Nevertheless, the spokesman had not finished.

"Have you not noticed the disappearance of about twenty-five of our brethren during the past two weeks? We still cannot account for it, except for the few whom the cats dragged away. The other traps are still there, not armed. Doesn't that make you think?" Now the university rat was imploring.

His hard-driving method was accomplishing more than any speech of Miguel would accomplish, much to Miguel's consternation.

"What is your final decision, brothers? Do we rush the farmhouse, or not?"

Spontaneously, and in unison they cried out, "No, no, no, no, no. No, no, no, no, no." And they continued with even greater intensity until the doorman once more cautioned them not to be so noisy.

"Very well, Mr. Chairman," he concluded. "What is your next point?"

Miguel nodded to Harold, this time with more confidence in him.

Harold pinned the second banner in place, also folded lengthwise through the middle. Then he lowered the folded half. There in bold letters was the slogan:

ROB AND STEAL, AND DON'T SAVE ANYTHING!

That was the last straw. The uproar was so great that the youngest cat began to stir from his slumber.

The doorman became quite urgent.

A venerable old rat, whose whiskers reached his chest, screamed, "More mouse propaganda! Let me question the author of these insults."

Harold stepped forward to the front of the platform, where they could see him better. With that the college graduate took his seat. The dim outside light cast an eerie shadow on the haystack behind.

"Young man, what do you mean by 'rob'?"

"Well, go into the farmhouse and take what belongs to the farmer."

"But we already voted not to do that."

The crowd shouted derisive statements at Harold, who was more than pleased. He did not want to appear tongue-in cheek, so he tried to think of something sad in order to sober himself. The fact was that he did not even know which direction the meeting was taking. Furthermore, even if he succeeded in teaching a valuable lesson, it was very improbable that the rats would give him credit for it. And something else: things were moving so rapidly that he did not have time to sort it all out. If anybody was learning, it was he. But he did not know what lesson he was learning. These thoughts passed through his mind as the rats shouted insults.

The delegation of tiny mice sat to the right of the platform as one faces the audience. They twitched and fidgeted. Since the meeting had already lasted more than an hour, they were drawing near to the end of their patience. The elderly mouse, Rudolf, had attended the convention expressly to give a speech but had not yet found the opportunity.

"Why should we not store up for another time. Don't men do it?" cried a rat.

"Yes! Yes! Yes! Yes! Yes! Yes! Yes! Yes!" the rats all screamed in unison. The sound of more than thirty rats all crying out at the same time was like the sound of a group of birds chattering, of chipmunks singing, or of the wind among brittle reeds. For the third time the guards ordered them to lower their voices.

Harold took advantage of the quiet to post his third and last banner, just as he had done with the other two. Unfolded, it read:

INSULT AND WOUND!

The rats were hardly prepared for that. The initial reaction was silence. The young self-appointed spokesman for the rats rushed up to the platform, but Rodolf did so at the same time. They almost collided in front of the podium. All—rats, mice, and worms alike—laughed at the spectacle. The mouse was like a miniature copy of the rat, but the rat had a more elongated, torpedo-like body. The rat, out of respect for age, stepped back.

Rudolf paused so long before speaking that his audience became uncomfortable. Then, talking with his teeth clenched and almost without moving his jaws, the mouse began. "What makes you such a stubborn clan? You have neither ancestry nor triumphs, but you insist on jeopardizing your own lives and ours!" On saying that he made wild gestures with his arms.

They pelted him with spit balls.

"What right have you to be offended when all of us suffer because of your self-interest?" He continued to talk with that clenched-mouth sarcasm.

When the younger rat could no longer stand it, he courteously asked the mouse to step aside. The gentleman became quite stiff and rigid and was not going to budge, but Miguel coaxed him to give in. He did so but with a great deal of muttering under his breath.

The young rat stood erect but with his head slightly bowed and with warm gestures, addressed the combined group.

"Brothers and friends," he began. "Bear with me, please. I realize I must hurry because we have almost reached the limits of the patience of mice and rats." He deliberately put the mice ahead of the rats because the "little people" were the more belligerent and stubborn even if the "big people" were admittedly more disorderly.

"We appreciate the loving efforts of the mice to help us, even how they keep telling us how they developed a system of storing food in order not to have to enter the man's house anymore. We understand all that."

The mice began to titter and to sway to and fro rhythmically as a visible sign of appreciation.

The spokesman for the rats resisted the temptation to mar his praise with negative comments. Both men and beasts find it difficult to do that. The seed in the Mouse Storehouse was beginning to sprout and it would not be long before the man got suspicious and dug it up. They would have to work fast and hard and hope it did not rain much during the next few days. He would await his opportunity and speak kindly with Miguel and Harold, who seemed to be the leaders of the mice in that community, at least, as soon as possible.

"We are sure our neighbors can comprehend why we are determined not to enter the farmhouse, why we will work and lay by. Our relative the pack rat has taught us some techniques too—even if we begin by storing away the children's rubber balls. And surely we all have enjoyed the praise with which I conclude this meeting. I am sure that all will agree that commendation is better than insulting and offending."

He had deliberately said that he was concluding the meeting, without so much as offering the chair to Miguel once again. It was ten till ten, and at the end of the two hours, tiny beasts release a bundle of energy which is in danger of consuming them and making them act with an indiscretion which possibly puts their life in danger. He clapped his paws, but they only saw him do it. At any rate, all began applauding, and their inaudible clapping lasted until ten o'clock sharp. Then instantaneously the rats disappeared into their holes and the mice looked for signs from the watchman to see if it was safe for them to return home.

Chapter Nine
Nobody Held the Meeting Together

The rats had been appeased. Time would tell what effect that would have on life on the farm. The fate of the three unhappy cats was also pending. Miguel suggested that they wait three days before trying to sort out the evidence. Because of the tension they had been under, they needed to rest anyway.

Byron burrowed down under the disabled motor vehicle which was under the shed beside the hen house and slept. He was fairly sure that no plow would catch him unawares there and cut him in two.

Harold and Cassandra were even more surprised to see their son when they returned from the meeting. You could hardly call him a teenager any longer. He was almost a man, who showed a keen interest in the meeting and asked many penetrating questions. They gave him a detailed description of the young pack rights advocate. When Timothy heard how the young statesman was dressed, he was overwhelmed with the kind of admiration which adolescents sometimes feel for young adults.

"For this I ran away from home," Cassandra lamented. "He grew up all too fast."

Harold had learned not to carry on conversation after remarks of that kind. No matter what he said, Cassandra would be offended. He just nodded his head and tried to make meaningful sounds. At the same time, both observed their son carefully for any signs of an apology for making their lives miserable. The truth was that Timothy did not remember any of it. In fact, in true animal fashion, even Harold and Cassandra's memories of these events were starting to fade.

On the third day Miguel arrived. Shortly thereafter Byron's knock was heard on the door. Before tea and cakes and rootbrew could be set on the table, Tillie and her husband, Rudolf arrived. They marveled over how Timothy had grown—in just four or five days.

"Before you know it, Cassandra," Tillie said, "He'll be getting married." She liked to provoke her friend.

"Too true, too true," Cassandra lamented, but she did not get tense like she had before. Harold was grateful for that. Tillie's words had pierced her heart like a dart, but Cassandra knew that she also had grown when she did not retort with, "At least I hope he doesn't marry a young rat!" Harold looked at her anxiously and had further reason to be grateful when she did not say it. Not only that, but Cassandra's feeling towards rats was beginning to mellow.

Instead, Cassandra did something which she would never have done before. She leaned over and, gently touching Tillie's hand, said, "Tillie, we are all indebted to you for your heroism."

"Heroism?" Tillie asked, giving herself certain airs, a mixture of both of importance and humility.

"Yes," Cassandra reaffirmed with genuine warmth. "You risked your life rather than give away the location of our granary..."

"Which is going to be discovered anyway because the seeds are sprouting and forming a dark green circle right where green should not be," Tillie completed Cassandra's statement. "I shudder every time I think about it. I almost felt that gray cat's breath on my tail."

Momentarily she was borne off in her mind to that awful instant and her short gray hairs stood straight up. Cassandra resisted the temptation to tell Tillie that she looked like a hedgehog when her hairs stood up like that.

"The mice are busy now transferring what seeds can be saved to another depot which is hopefully outside the cats' territory," Rudolf answered as he put his arm around his wife and held her tight. While Harold and Cassandra only had one, Rudolf and Tillie had five small ones at home and more on the way. Their family was so extensive that their family tree covered one entire wall of their apartment.

"It's inevitable that the farmer find out about our storehouse, and surely he will dig it up. However, the important thing is that no mice or rats be seen for a long time," Miguel said as a way of officially starting the meeting. "The rats haven't been seen since the meeting, and under the leadership of that outstanding young 'statesman,' as I like to call him, they've begun their plans too. But they're secretive about it. They don't want anyone to know where they're building nor how. My scouts tell me they're busy, but they can't get close enough to bring me any information."

All sat quietly meditating on the importance of those events.

Miguel broke the silence. "It appears that everything will turn out well in spite of Harold's slogans. Harold, what on earth made you think of inciting the rats to do exactly what we did not want them to do?"

Harold laughed and rather than try to justify himself, he actually heard himself say, "You're right, Miguel. What I did was risky and I think you already know why I did it. However, all of us—mice, worms, and rats—are indebted to you for the way you held the meeting together."

Then he held his breath because in reality nobody had held the meeting together, unless it had been the diplomatic rat. However, to his relief, Miguel was not apparently offended. Cassandra went to the kitchen to bring more tea and cakes.

Cassandra and Harold now understood what Miguel had intended to do and why Harold was concerned that it was impossible. No animal can compliment another. He had been sure of that. In fact, animals can do what humans long to do but cannot: insult each other with offensive names such as, "pig," "dog," "rat," "worm," "mouse", "fox," "chicken," and "skunk." Furthermore, they can add a string of qualifying words such as "fat," "mangy," "filthy," "sly," "sticky-tongued," "thievish," and "slothful" without anybody's really feeling anything. It is true that animals will growl and snarl, but humans aim missiles after similar insults. This knowledge is what had made Harold cynical about the idea.

Happily, Miguel accepted the compliment unconditionally.

"Life is funny," Cassandra mused. "We went to teach the rats how to store their food, but they probably knew that phase one of our project was failing. The seeds are sprouting. The farmer will know something. We'll have to find another place and hope to learn from the experience." Her laughter revealed true mirth and a light spirit. She was actually enjoying not harboring animosity against the rats. It made Harold feel good to see his wife like that.

Byron had been silent until then. Then he sat on the sofa beside Timothy and began sipping the tea that Cassandra had made. Each time she improved its flavor somewhat. One time it had a mint flavor. Another time it was like chamomile. Another time it tasted like sassafras.

He had been reflecting on his desire to be treated like a man and not like a worm even though he definitely did not want to be human. The very conversation with Harold which had triggered Cassandra's reaction had warmed his heart. He had crawled sadly out of the mouse house turning that question over in his mind. The answer would help him determine his purpose in life.

"The rats have changed and are changing more and more from day to day," he commented. "I know where they're building the granary and what methods they're using," he said.

"You do? Where?" Miguel jumped to his feet, slightly irritated because the worm knew something that was so important to him.

"Yes, I know, but I mustn't tell you," he said resolutely. "I found out, nosing around you might say." He laughed. He certainly did push a lot of dirt around with his nose.

"You're on our side, Byron," said Miguel, trying to pressure him into talking. However, Byron would not let himself be intimidated by the mouse. If he wanted to be treated like a man, human, he had to act like one. He would be loyal to the rats. They knew him and trusted him.

"Miguel, why is it important to you to know where the rats have made their barn. Why do you need to know?" He remained firm.

Miguel could not answer immediately. Then he said, "To advise them on how to do it well."

However, his answer had no weight to it because the mice's own storehouse had its flaws, and Miguel knew that Byron knew it.

"That's right, Miguel," Harold interrupted. "What is it we wanted to do? Encourage the rats to have a little self-respect, or tell them how to do their work?"

Miguel stammered a little. "Both. No? If they learned from us, wouldn't that help them to have self-respect?" He looked rather nervously around from one to the other. The effects of the meeting were only beginning to reach home. It was a lot harder for him to recognize the rats' good qualities than he had realized. The animal instinct was deeply embedded in him.

"But why have we failed?" Miguel cried out at last. "The idea was a good one, wasn't it?" he asked, looking from one to another again. "Harold, you're the one who couldn't pay a compliment."

"I know it," replied Harold without lowering his glance.

"Why is it so difficult to like them?" lamented Miguel. "The truth is my heart is closed. If I found their hideaway, I'm sure I would immediately begin insulting them."

Byron observed all this with wonder. "I overheard the rats talking. They said they had disciplined the young rats who played soccer with the cat. Each one will have to do additional construction—hard labor—because their folly almost resulted in disaster for all of us." He said that as he hovered over the cup of tea.

"Cassandra," he said, "every pot you brew is more delicious that the one before."

"I'm glad, Byron," she said, genuinely delighted, and she disappeared into the kitchen to bring more treats.

Byron was beginning to understand himself better. The good thing was that nobody stood out as a hero. His deep conversation with Harold had to do with why animals feel frustrated at times. It is when they are prevented by circumstances from being what they are supposed to be. For example, he could not believe that rats were made to live in barns. But since they have to live in barns, like cattle, who should be surprised if they act, not like cattle exactly but, like frustrated animals?

Were he a psychologist, he might be able to help them. He began to visualize his office under a weeping willow with office hours posted on a stone. He could advise all kinds of animals, but on separate days, of course. Rabbits and foxes could not come on the same day. No, no, why even consider it?

Abruptly he ended his reverie. His role was to lighten the soil along with billions of other earthworms the world over. Humans say if it were not for the earthworms, the ground would be untillable, hard as stone. He would set his heart to it as soon as possible. Probably he would transfer to the field where the farmer was to sow wheat. Wheat was used to produce flour. Flour was used to make bread to feed those who felt hungry, be they poor or rich. He felt sad because he would be too far from Harold and his family to visit them often.

However, Harold helped him to make his decision.

"Friends," he said, beaming with pride. "Little Timothy is not so little anymore. And now he's going to have to make room for others. Cassandra and I want you to know that she's expecting. This time it looks like we're going to have four!"

Tillie got up from her seat and embraced Cassandra. "Oh, Cassandra," she wept, "may our children be born on the same day so your boys can marry my girls.

Cassandra squeezed her tightly. "I hope it's exactly as you say, Tillie."

Whether out of jealousy or because he remembered how he had been until a short while ago, Timothy felt weak in the knees. His soft fur appeared moist with perspiration.

Tillie's husband, Rudolf noticed and patted him on the shoulder. "Don't worry, Timmy. You'll get over it. I felt that way once when my younger brothers were born. But you'll be married before you know it and will have children of your own." He smiled to reassure Timothy, but deep and mysterious feelings were frightening the young mouse.

Byron remembered how Timothy had been, even if Timothy himself did not. And he knew that, at least for three months, he did not want to be a visitor in Harold Mouse's house. That would be late summer or early fall, practically the end of his hardest work.

Chapter Ten
It Always Takes Time to See Progress

It always takes time to see progress. By the end of the summer it was becoming clear in what the meeting with the rats would result. First of all, the farmer got rid of the three cats and brought back the first one, who was quite happy to be home. For several days he strutted around the backyard of the house to announce that he was home again, and king! Nevertheless, because there was no evidence of the presence of rats and mice on the property, the farmer's wife began feeding the animal. From day to day he grew fatter and fatter and started taking several long naps each day. He was so regular that the small animals got to know his schedule. Still, they moved about with great care.

The rats, unable to distinguish between the "good" boxes and the "bad" (that is, the traps that did not look like traps), gave orders to their people not to go near any box at all. Really, there was no need for them to do so, since their cache was on the edge of the wood that circled the farm. Cautiously, they planned access routes arriving from different places so that traffic would not be heavy along the way. Some of the younger and more adventurous of the band were assigned to colonize the wooded area to avoid overcrowding in the barn.

Soon the rats discerned what would be their challenge: Ants. These "animalcules" who invented the cellular telephone send out scouts within a wide radius of their colony. Once they discover food, they "telephone" back and soon a hoard of invaders shows up. If moisture put a damper on the mice's venture, the ever-present ants did so on the rats'. Time would tell if the rats succeeded in negotiating with the ants, as the mice had tried to do with the rats. During the time covered by this account, no solution had been found. At any rate, the final results do not belong to this story.

Another chapter was being written in the field which Felix had set aside for wheat. Byron and a host of his relatives had burrowed down, being careful to avoid the discs of the plow. When the vibrations warned them, they simply dug down deeper. Roger was the most difficult case. He had the "nobody-tells-me-what-to-do" mentality so deeply ingrained in him that his cousins had to hold on to his tail to keep him from going up when the plow passed along instead of going down deeper.

In the rich, loamy earth, which the worms made richer, they were in their element. One day the farmer sowed seed. Later, the worms felt the roots trickling down like dew. The few rootlets they snipped off to make tea did not impair the growth of the plants. The pruning probably helped them to grow. The wheat grew tall and green. Then, one day it began to turn golden.

The worms listened as Felix admired his work. Although he never failed to give recognition to the "lowly earthworm," they did not let that bother them. At first Roger talked of revenge for the insult, but his cousins convinced him that against the iron blades of the plow he was no match.

"Roger, you're a fine young man," they told him constantly. "You've got to live no matter what others think about you. And why should other people's remarks diminish your happiness? Forget that about being "lowly." In a way, we are "lowly" because we live down low in the ground," said a wise old worm.

"Nor are we like canaries," said a mature woman. "When I lived in the flower garden, I got to know what a canary is. I don't know if they are more beautiful than we are or not. Men say so. But I don't know if I agree with them. Think about this, Roger: Canaries cannot work, but we can. If their owner forgets to feed them, they suffer. True, they don't eat worms, but if they escape from their cages, they are never seen again because they don't know how to work."

From day to day they comforted Roger, and Byron began to see how noble Miguel's idea was, even though it had not been apparent in the great meeting. Great ideas have to flourish and gain acceptance. Man and beast received benefits from the earthworms' hard work. The farmer became more pacific because he was going to reap a bountiful harvest. Even though he never changed his story about the traveling people and the tracks in the earth, he made no new accusations against others.

The good results even reached as far as the fowl. The mother of the duck who had wanted to make Cassandra her pet got to hear of her daughter's idle talk, and she felt disgusted. Even though she lived on the neighboring farm, she had freedom to move around, for ducks like to seek water. One day she showed up just as her daughter was beginning to bore the other fowl with a word-by-word repetition of her experience with the mouse. She never varied a single expression. If she inadvertently changed a word, she apologized and repeated the whole account up to the point where she digressed.

She had arrived at the part about wanting to pick the mouse by the tail when her mother, with a loud squawk, corrected her.

"Hortense, what's this I've been hearing about you? I had to leave a hen sitting on my eggs to pay a visit since I will be quite busy for some while now."

Hortense looked down. No answer came out of her bill.

"Your father's green head would turn gray if he were around to hear what you've been saying." The mother duck folded her wings akimbo and paced about. Hortense's father, as the barnyard fowl say, had been invited by the farmer's family to a roast duck dinner. Afterwards, the mother had married again. However, she always taught her children to respect the dignity of other animals and not to peck mice's tails.

"How quickly you've forgotten your upbringing!"

Hortense felt humiliated because, after all, she was an adult and no longer lived under her mother's wing. Nevertheless, the fiery mallard continued. "How is that poor little mouse to feel when she knows you keep talking about her humiliation?"

"How is she to know?" Hortense protested.

"Because your neighbors and the other animals talk. She hears what things you say about her," the mother answered. "What was her name, if you wanted her as a pet," the mother challenged, rising up on tip toes.

"I don't know. I called her Froggy," answered the abashed Hortense.

"That's what the other animals told me," replied the mother. "Froggy? But didn't you know she was a mouse?"

"Well, yes, but—" Hortense felt her mouth going dry. "I thought it would be cute to give her a, well, you know, a nickname."

"But why change her identity? She couldn't be a frog if she worked at it the rest of her life!"

Mother Duck, it seemed, had the same inflexibility that her daughter had. Since she had about reached the limit of her repertory, soon she would be repeating the same questions over and over until the other fowls were completely beside themselves.

The rooster, who was supposedly the head of the house, began to wonder if he should restore order to his house.

However, Hortense, influenced by the recent developments on the farm, was moved to say: "Mother, I know it wasn't easy for you to come all the way from where you live with the babies and all..." She spoke slowly and deliberately to let her words sink in. The hens listened with interest.

The mother mallard was visibly touched. That was the first time any of her children had commended her. A tear began to form in her eye.

"And believe me, Mother, I saw you in my mind's eye when I was with that tiny creature." She paused.

"You did?" replied the mother, flabbergasted.

"Yes, and you were telling me not to mistreat any fellow animal."

"Then why did you pick her up by the tail?" asked the mother duck, bewildered.

Hortense paused a long while. "I didn't pick her up by the tail. Don't you understand me? I remembered my home training."

"But you were going to take her away from her husband and son and keep her here in the henhouse as your pet, your slave." The mother's tone was more pleading now, rather than demanding.

"Why?" Hortense asked rhetorically. "Why would I do that?" The rooster and the hens cocked their heads to one side to hear the answer.

"You taught me to respect the dignity of all animals, but you never explained what that entailed," explained the distraught duck. "How was I to know what my limits were? I'm sorry," she said. "I'm just so sorry." Hortense's eyes filled with tears. She and her mother wrapped their wings around one another and kissed each other with a sweeping motion of the bill across the cheek. After that, Mother Duck waddled away to return to her nest.

Harold and Cassandra were truly happy. In time, they had four more children and before long, these were filling the house with their frantic antics. However, Harold and Cassandra were emotionally prepared this time. Knowing that the pressure would only last a short while comforted them. Timothy was willing to continue living at home and help with the education of his younger siblings.

He would sit with them on the porch of their little house and point out to them the activities and personalities of the barnyard.

He drilled them on the cat's schedule for sleeping and inculcated in them that they must never go near a live cat, even while he is sleeping.

Cassandra and Harold were so happy to have Timothy

at home that they constructed a little room for him on the side of the parlor, because the quadruplets had put him out of his room. His younger brothers and sisters did not bother him so much because he was busy working with Miguel on his chronicle.

Epilogue

I feel rather frustrated, and even angry, that I did not receive the credit for the success of the Animal Congress. I feel rather out of sorts with Timothy Mouse also because he knows how to re-write the story of all that happened on Farmer Felix's place. In fact, I am almost sure that he has already completed the manuscript. Recently we moved our offices to the hollow trunk of an old elm tree which is near the farmhouse. The upper branches overhang the roof. There are many nooks and crannies where I can hide scraps of paper to use if I ever get a brilliant idea. At times I send Timothy out on pointless errands just to get him out so I can search for his work. I know he has done it! I know it is there! But until now he has successfully hidden it from me.

At times, I try to provoke him into an argument, but his grammar is flawless. To speak in defense of or against the rats is no longer to speak of current events. It would be like getting angry over disagreements between Romans and Scythians. Who cares anymore?

One day when I was especially vexed, I shouted at him, "What keeps me from writing the history which would make me famous?"

He gave me his, "I don't have social antennas" grin and headed out of the room.

"I guess it's you," he said and closed the door.

Miguel Bukmas, 20__

Author's Note

The main purpose of this story is to entertain. Any who think they see profound or hidden symbolisms have seen more than the author imagined. The book is not intended to be scientific. Some, if not many, of the statements about the different species are as fantastical as the fact that the animals in the story speak to one another and understand human speech. The different animal groups are not intended to represent or symbolize any ethnic or national groups, past, present, or future.

Although at the end of the story a certain peace prevailed on the farm, this is no Utopian tale. The animals are still animals, and the humans are completely untouched by and even unaware of all that has happened on their farm.

At times it may be therapeutic for us imperfect beings to laugh at the foibles and idosyncracies of mankind. Nevertheless, for the answer to all human problems, we have to turn to the Bible, not to a work of fiction.